Ladybird books are widely available, but in case of difficulty may be ordered by post or telephone from:
Ladybird Books – Cash Sales Department Littlegate Road Paignton Devon TQ3 3BE Telephone 0803 554761

A catalogue record for this book is available from the British Library

Published by Ladybird Books Ltd Loughborough Leicestershire UK
LADYBIRD and the device of a Ladybird are trademarks of Ladybird Books Ltd

Disney

Winnie the Pooh's
Christmas

Ladybird

It was the night before Christmas, and the snow fell softly on the Hundred Acre Wood.

Pooh stood gazing out of the window. "I'm very glad to see you," he chuckled to the plump snowflakes drifting past.

Pooh turned to take a look at the decorations filling his home. "Let me see," he thought, "a tree, some candles…" Pooh scratched his head and sighed. "There seems to be something missing!"

All at once Pooh heard a gentle tap at his front door. "Perhaps," Pooh smiled to himself, "that is whatever it is that's missing!"

Pooh opened the door to find a very small snowman with a pair of very Piglet-looking ears.

"Oh!" remarked Pooh, who was a very surprised little bear. Then he added, "Hello!" to be polite, because one should always be polite, even to surprises.

"H-H-Hello, P-Pooh B-Bear," the snowman answered in a very Piglet-sounding voice. "M-Merry Christmas!"

Pooh wondered whether it was more polite to invite the snowman in where it was warm, or to let him stay outside where snowmen are usually more comfortable. The snowman finally gave Pooh a very small hint. "May I come in?" it asked.

"Please do," said Pooh.

The snowman hurried inside and stood in front of the fire. "The only thing I don't like about Christmas," said the snowman, "and it's a very small thing, is that my ears get so very cold."

"I can imagine," replied Pooh, who could not imagine a snowman's ears being anything *but* cold.

The snowman stood shivering in front of the fire, and with every tremble and quiver began to look less and less like a snowman and more and more like Piglet!

"Why, hello, Piglet!" blurted Pooh, delighted to see his very small, very best friend standing in a puddle of water on the hearth where, just moments before, a snowman had stood. "If I had known it was you, I would have invited you in!"

Piglet smiled up at his friend. "Oh, Pooh! You *did* invite me in. You knew it was me all along!"

"Well, of course I did, Piglet," responded Pooh, scratching his head. "I just didn't know I knew until this particular moment."

"My!" breathed Piglet in wonder as he gazed up at Pooh's Christmas tree, glimmering golden in the candlelight. Dozens of candles hung from its branches, each nestling in its own honey pot. "I've never seen so many candles on one tree."

"Well," explained Pooh, "there seemed to be a great many empty honey pots to use as candle holders. And there was a great deal of extra room on the tree because the popcorn didn't seem to get strung."

"Shall I help you string the popcorn?" asked Piglet.

"Why, yes, Piglet. I'd like that very much," Pooh answered. "That is, if there were any popcorn left to string, which there isn't."

"Oh dear," said Piglet, nervously. "What happened to it all?"

"I ate it," Pooh whispered back. "I was tasting it to make sure it was properly popped, and by the time I was sure," Pooh shrugged and sighed, "it was all gone. I do, however, still have the string."

"That's all right, Pooh!" Piglet laughed. "We can use the string to wrap your presents!"

"But, Piglet," chuckled Pooh, "the gifts won't be here until tomorrow morning. And then I *unwrap* them." Pooh leant close and whispered confidentially into Piglet's ear, "That's the way it's done, you know."

There may have been a few things about Christmas on which Pooh was a little hazy, but opening presents wasn't one of them.

"No, Pooh," said Piglet, "I mean I'll help you wrap the presents you're going to *give!*"

Pooh's smile disappeared. "Oh!" he said quietly. "*Those* gifts." Then even more quietly he added, "Oh bother!"

"What's the matter, Pooh?" Piglet asked.

Pooh sighed heavily. "I think I just remembered what I forgot," he said. "Presents."

"No presents?" Piglet looked up at Pooh sadly. "Not even a very small one?"

Pooh shook his head. He hated seeing his little friend so unhappy. "I'm sorry, Piglet."

Piglet smiled bravely. "It's all right, Pooh. I always get a bit too excited about presents. And it's the thought that counts, you know," he sniffed.

"Now, if you don't mind, I think I'll take my very cold ears and go home."

Pooh saw his friend to the door and watched him walk
sadly down the path as the snowflakes began to turn him
into a very small snowman once again.

Pooh stepped out into the snow. "I think I'd better ask Christopher Robin what *he* thinks about thoughts and presents and Christmas and everything," he said.

It was a long, chilly walk through the snowy night. The snowflakes tickled Pooh's nose and crept down the back of his neck to get warm. He was very glad when he arrived at Christopher Robin's house, and knocked loudly on the door.

"Pooh Bear!" Christopher Robin exclaimed. "What a wonderful surprise! Come in!"

Pooh was led into Christopher Robin's cosy room, glowing with candlelight from a large Christmas tree.

"My!" Pooh breathed. "This certainly looks like Christmas! So I suppose I can ask you what I came to find out."

He rubbed his chin thoughtfully. "As soon as I remember what it is."

But then Pooh frowned and stepped up to Christopher Robin's fireplace, where a row of socks and stockings of all shapes and sizes hung neatly from the mantelpiece.

"Don't you think," Pooh remarked, trying to look as wise as possible, "that Christmas is, perhaps, not the best time for drying your washing?"

"Silly Old Bear," Christopher Robin laughed, ruffling the fluff on Pooh's head. "That's not washing. They're stockings to hold Christmas presents!"

"You mean," Pooh answered slowly, trying to take it all in, "you have to have stockings to put presents in?"

"Yes," said Christopher Robin, "that's the way it's done."

"Oh bother!" said Pooh, looking down at his feet. Not only did he have no presents for his friends, but they had no stockings to put their presents in! Pooh, being a bear, had little use for stockings. Bare feet are, after all, something which bears are used to. All Pooh's friends in the Hundred Acre Wood were much the same way.

When Pooh mentioned this, Christopher Robin laughed. "Come with me, Pooh. I have plenty of stockings for *everyone*."

Christopher Robin showed Pooh a drawer containing socks and stockings of every size, shape and colour.

"These are all stockings that have lost their mates and would love to have someone with whom to share Christmas," said Christopher Robin. He scratched one of Pooh's ears. "It's the thought that counts, you know."

"Why, yes," replied Pooh, pleased that his friend had remembered to answer the question he had forgotten to ask. "Thank you very much, Christopher Robin."

Soon Pooh was walking happily home with his arms full of stockings. The snow had stopped falling, leaving a wonderful white blanket over the entire forest. It was as if, the Hundred Acre Wood had decorated itself for Christmas. A huge moon made it seem as bright as day.

"But," Pooh reminded himself with a yawn, "it is very late, and I must get these stockings delivered." He considered for a moment. "I must get everyone presents, too, of course, but the stockings come first."

And so Pooh, being as quiet as the soft night around him, crept into his friends' homes, one by one, and hung up a stocking—each with a little note, which read, *FROM POOH*.

First, of course,
there was Piglet's
house, where Pooh
placed a very small
stocking on a nail.

He then left a
striped one for
Tigger, because
he was sure that
was the sort of
stocking that
Tiggers like best.

Pooh left a very
bright orange one
at Rabbit's house.

Eeyore got the
warmest and
friendliest stocking
Pooh could find.

Gopher received
a long, dark
stocking. Pooh
thought it was what
a tunnel would look
like if a tunnel
were a stocking.

Finally, Owl was given
a stocking the colour
of the sky – in which,
Pooh thought, he
would like to fly if
he were Owl.

It was very, very late when Pooh nailed his own honey-coloured stocking to his very own mantelpiece.

"Now that this stocking business is all taken care of," said Pooh, settling down in his softest armchair, "I must do some serious thinking about what I am going to give my friends for Christmas." Pooh closed his eyes, and soon neither his snoring nor the sun rising over the Hundred Acre Wood disturbed his thoughts.

In fact, Pooh did not stop his deep thinking, or loud snoring, until a knock sounded at his door, accompanied by a chorus of "Merry Christmas, Pooh!"

Pooh opened his eyes and looked up at the clock. He'd been asleep for hours!

"Oh, no!" he thought. "My friends are here for Christmas and I have no presents for any of them! There's only one thing to do," he told himself sternly. "I shall simply have to tell my friends I'm sorry, but I only *thought* about presents for them."

Pooh opened his door and started to apologize, but before he could say a word, in rushed all his friends—Piglet, Tigger, Rabbit, Gopher, Eeyore and Owl—all thanking Pooh at once for his thoughtful gifts.

Piglet was wearing a new stocking cap. "My ears are very grateful, Pooh. It's exactly what I wanted."

Tigger told Pooh how much he loved his new 'stripedy' sleeping bag. "It's cosier than cosy!" he cried, bouncing and trouncing with joy.

Rabbit couldn't wait to tell Pooh how he'd always dreamed of owning a colour-coordinated carrot cover. How could Pooh possibly have known?

Gopher thanked
Pooh for the bag
to collect his rock
samples in. "Never
had one big enough
before!" he said.

Eeyore explained—
if anyone was
interested—that his
tail had never been
warmer than in its
new warmer.

Owl was certain his brand-new 'wind-sock' would provide him with all the information he needed to prevent the occasional crash-landing through his dining-room window!

Pooh put his hands behind his back and looked thoughtful. "Something awfully nice is going on, but I'm not sure what!" he said.

"I'll tell you what it is, Pooh," exclaimed Tigger. "It's Christmas!" He pushed a large pot of honey into Pooh's stocking.

"And this is for you, too," said Owl, handing over his present.
The others quickly followed suit with presents of their own –
which all turned out to be pots of honey.

Well, what else would a Pooh Bear want for Christmas…
or any other time?

"Christmas," sighed Pooh happily. "What a very sweet thought indeed!"